For James, Tabitha, Leo and Henry.

A long time ago, a clockmaker called Hans lived in a
mountain village. He worked from dawn until far into the
night, making and repairing clocks and watches.

His tools hung on the wall above his bench,
but the shelves on the other walls were filled
with clocks and watches of all kinds, some
to be repaired, and some that
Hans had made to sell.

The largest of them all, a fine grandfather clock that showed day and night, and the seasons as well as the time, stood in the corner opposite the door, so that anyone who came in could see its magnificence.

Early in the morning as the sun rose over the mountain peaks, Hans dressed
and went out into the cobbled street, locking his door behind him.
Every morning, Yani the goatherd drove his herd of goats pattering through
the village, their bells chiming as they skipped and jostled each other.

When they stopped to drink at the fountain in the centre of the square, Hans strode past, glancing up at the church clock he had made. He hurried into the baker's shop, bought his bread for the day, and without a word to anyone, strode back to his workshop.

'He's strange,' the villagers said to one another. 'Never a 'good morning' or a 'how are you?' No friends, no family, what a lonely life!'

FISHMONGER

BAKERY

One spring when the snow on the lower slopes had melted and flowers sprinkled the new grass, Hans started work on a clock he had designed. It was a clock with bell chimes and carved flowers and would need many hours of work to finish. The hands of the little clock were lacy gold.

The case was made from cherry wood, carved and polished.

'I wish I had more time,' Hans muttered as he toiled, and the hours ticked by. 'I'll sell this clock for lots of money. I need more time to make more like it.'

Hans decided he wouldn't go to bed until the clock was finished. He worked until evening came and he had to light the candles. Then he ate his last bread roll and worked on, while the light faded, and the stars appeared over the village.

'If I had more time, I could make a dozen of these clocks instead of repairing people's pocket watches,' he muttered. 'I would be rich. If only I had more time!'

He moved the
candles closer.

There was a
loud knocking!

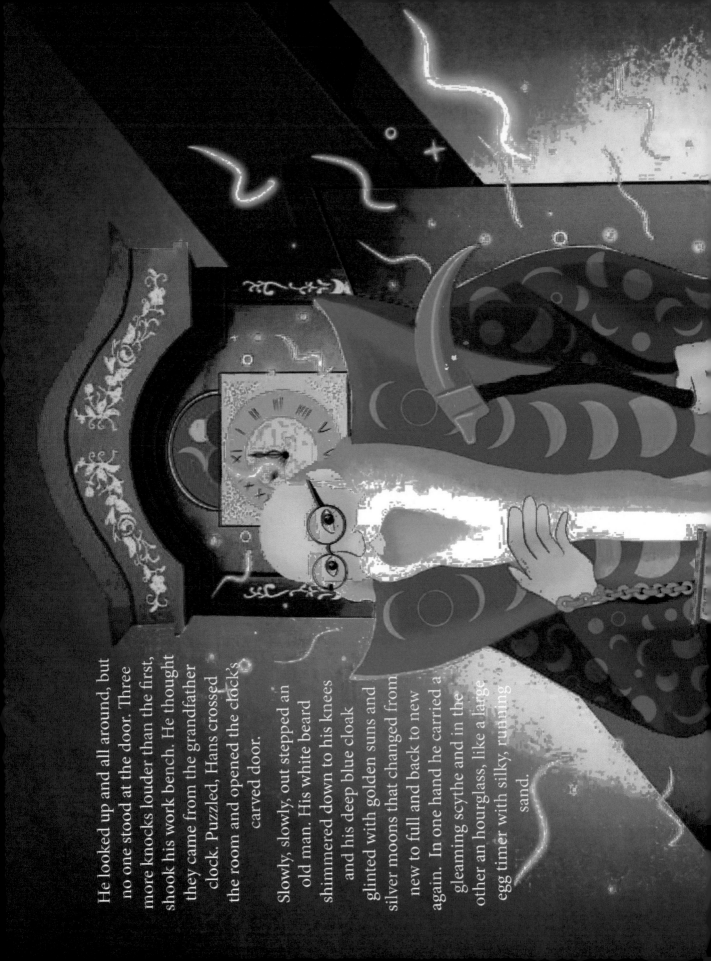

He looked up and all around, but no one stood at the door. Three more knocks louder than the first, shook his work bench. He thought they came from the grandfather clock. Puzzled, Hans crossed the room and opened the clock's carved door.

Slowly, slowly, out stepped an old man. His white beard shimmered down to his knees and his deep blue cloak glinted with golden suns and silver moons that changed from new to full and back to new again. In one hand he carried a gleaming scythe and in the other an hourglass, like a large egg timer with silky, running sand.

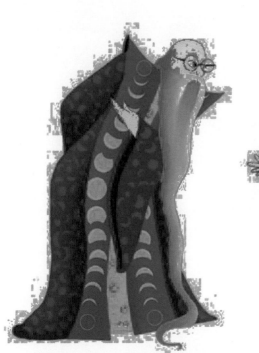

Hans's heart skipped and raced, but he knew who the old man was. 'Father Time!' he exclaimed.

Father Time bowed and smiled. 'I think you wanted me,' he said.

'Well, yes,' said Hans. 'At least, I wanted more time.'

'For what?' asked Father Time.

'So that I can make more money,' replied Hans.

Father Time laughed. 'I thought you might ask for more rest,' he said, 'or for more time with your wife and children.'

'I have no wife, nor children,' snapped Hans. 'I don't want them. They would cost me money for clothes and food, and I don't have enough money now.'

'But you could teach your children to make clocks,' said Father Time, raising one bushy eyebrow.

'No, I couldn't,' said Hans. 'They'd take my trade.'

Father Time stared at him, his old eyes gleaming. Then he smiled. 'Very well,' he said, nodding. 'From midnight tonight, I shall stop time for everyone else. Then you can have as much of it as you want. We'll see how well you do with it!'

'Thank you,' Hans said, astonished. 'That will be very useful.'

Father Time smiled again and turning, stepped back into the grandfather clock and shut the door.

Hans settled down to work straightaway, noticing that it was only two hours to midnight.

He didn't feel tired anymore, and he smiled as he thought of the work he could do while everyone else was asleep.

The clocks in the workshop ticked away, chiming the quarter and half hours,

eleven o'clock,

quarter past eleven,

half past eleven,

a quarter to twelve,

until at last, they came to midnight. Hans held his breath.

On the first stroke of midnight, ever¬
clock in the room stopped. Hans
breathed again, and the only sound
was his breath. In the enormous
silence, he tiptoed about, feeling the
stillness around him. Only the candl¬
flames flickered as he passed, making
his shadow waver on the walls.

Then he started work again.
The little clock was almost
finished, and its charm grew
under his fingers. He thought
of nothing else until one of
the candles burnt out.

'Bother!' said Hans and moved another
one closer so that he could see his work.
Then he noticed that they were all
burning low, so he went to the
cupboard to find more. There were only
two left.
'Never mind,' he said to himself. 'I can
buy some tomorrow,' and he glanced
at the clocks. Every clock in the room
stood at midnight.

'Oh!' he exclaimed. 'Well never mind;
I can use one candle at a time,' and he
snuffed all the candles but one, and set
that one close to him.

He worked until all the candles were burnt out except one. He
peered anxiously out the window. The sky was dark.
'What shall I do?' he wondered. 'There aren't any more candles.'
It was then that he realised how tired he was. His back
ached, his eyes ached, and his fingers were sore.
'Never mind,' he told himself again. 'I shall feel better if I have
breakfast and then I'll decide what to do. The baker bakes early.'

He put on his coat and stepped into the silent street. There was no one about. Down in the square the fountain was still. Hans stared at it. The tiny water droplets hung in cascades of motionless crystals, like a fairy fountain made of ice that glittered in the moonlight.

Hans shook his head and moved on. In the darkness he couldn't see the hands of the church clock, but he knew they pointed to midnight. He crossed the square to the baker's shop, but before he reached it, he knew it was as still as the rest of the village. The baker and his wife were asleep. The bakery was dark, and the ovens were cold.

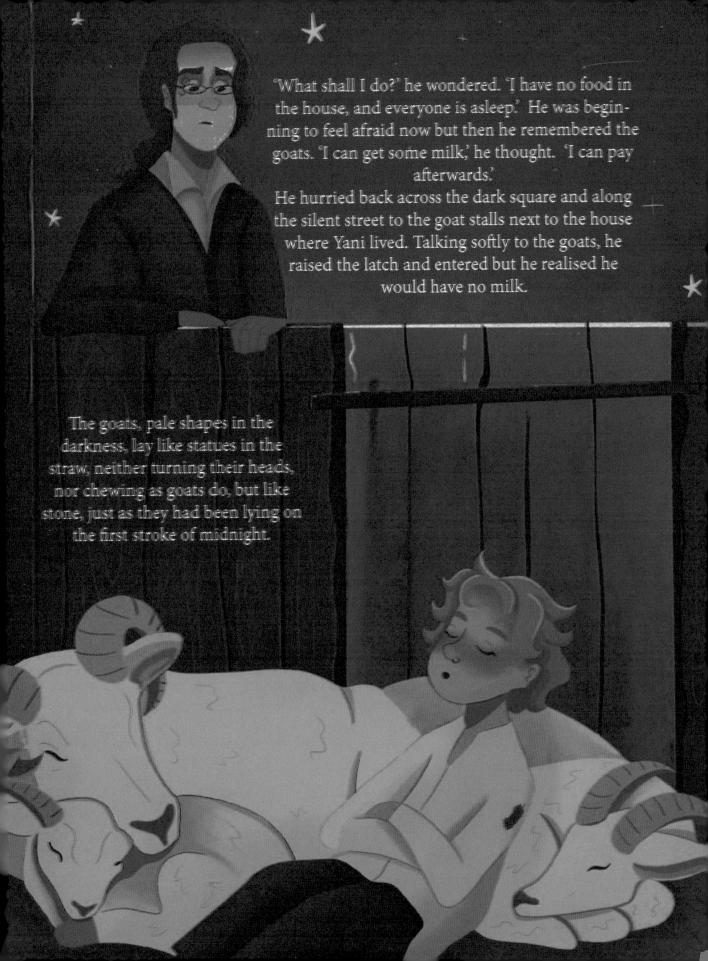

'What shall I do?' he wondered. 'I have no food in the house, and everyone is asleep.' He was beginning to feel afraid now but then he remembered the goats. 'I can get some milk,' he thought. 'I can pay afterwards.'

He hurried back across the dark square and along the silent street to the goat stalls next to the house where Yani lived. Talking softly to the goats, he raised the latch and entered but he realised he would have no milk.

The goats, pale shapes in the darkness, lay like statues in the straw, neither turning their heads, nor chewing as goats do, but like stone, just as they had been lying on the first stroke of midnight.

Hans closed the door and returned to his home trying not to be afraid. How could he see to work in the dark? How could he buy food and candles and milk when the shops would not open, and the goats slept forever?

He stumbled into his workshop telling himself not to think about it, making up his mind to light the last candle and finish his beautiful clock. In his work he forgot his fears, and although he grew hungrier and colder, at last the clock was finished.

He sat back to admire it in the dim candlelight and then opened the little door at the back to set it going.
It wouldn't go! No matter how he set and swung the tiny pendulum, the hands stuck at twelve o'clock.

Hans stared at it, not seeing the elegant figures on the face, nor the glossy flowers and birds carved around it, but only hands that would never move and bells that would never chime.

'Oh no, oh no, oh no,' he wailed. 'What's the point of making a beautiful clock that won't work?' He sunk his head in his hands and wept. He was cold, worn out, hungry, afraid, and all his efforts on his little clock were useless. Besides, who could buy the clock when they were all asleep?

'Oh, I am a fool!' Hans moaned. 'I didn't realise how I needed everyone.'
He stumbled to the grandfather clock and drummed on the door with his fists
'Father Time! Father Time!' he cried. 'Please come back! I've made a terrible mistake. Father Time!'

He hammered again on the door.

Slowly, slowly, the door opened and out stepped Father Time. The sand in his hourglass was still. Father Time smiled. 'What was your mistake? 'he asked.

'I know now that nothing works if you stop time,' said Hans. 'The baker doesn't bake, and the goats don't give milk and my clock won't go, and there's no one to buy it and I'm tired and hungry.'

'So, you have learned the lesson,' said Father Time, nodding. 'Clocks only tell us the time. They don't make it. There must be day and night and work and rest. Everyone must have time. If they don't there will be no bread, no candles, no goats' milk and no customers for your clocks.'

'I know that now,' whispered the clockmaker. 'I hadn't thought before.'

Father Time raised a long thin finger. 'Remember,' he said, 'that there must be a time for everything.' Then he tapped the hourglass, the sand flowed, and every clock in the workshop chimed the second stroke of midnight. As the clocks counted their way to twelve, Father time turned and stepped back into the grandfather clock. By the time the sounds died away, he was gone.

But Time was not.

All the clocks ticked on. Hans pulled his stool to the window, wrapped a coat around his cold limbs, and waited. He didn't work, and he didn't sleep. He counted the hours as they ticked through the longest night of all until the first rays of the rising sun lit the mountain peaks above the steep slopes.

As the light flooded the valley and touched the rooftops of the village, Hans stepped out into the street again, and here were the goats trotting along the cobble-stones, murmuring and bleating to one another as they came, while behind them singing and twirling a stick sauntered Yani.

'Good morning Yani' called Hans strolling beside him. 'What a fine morning!'

Yani stared. 'It is Sir. I – it is,' he stuttered, and watched in amazement as Hans patted two of the goats when they paused to drink at the fountain.

'Perhaps I should buy a goat,' said Hans, rubbing the soft ears of a tawny kid as it nostled its mother. 'If I did, would you graze it for me and teach me how to milk it? And would your mother make cheese for me?'

Yani's jaw dropped but then he grinned. 'Yes, of course,' he replied. 'Of course we would!'

'Good, good. I'll do that then. And Yani, please could you bring me some milk tonight?'

'The very best,' said Yani.

'Thank you!' called Hans, and he strode on, past the church with its bright clock on the tower, its gleaming golden hands pointing at last to seven o'clock, and on across the square towards the baker's shop, and the smell of fresh baked bread.

Printed in Great Britain
by Amazon